How to Knit a Monster

How to Knit a Monster

by Annemarie van Haeringen

CLARION BOOKS
Houghton Mifflin Harcourt | Boston New York

CLARION BOOKS
3 Park Avenue, New York, New York 10016

Copyright © 2014 by Annemarie van Haeringen
First published in the Netherlands in 2014 by Uitgeverij Leopold,
Wibautstraat 133, 1097 DN Amsterdam under the title *Sneeuwwitje breit een monster*.
First published in the United States in 2018 by Clarion Books.

Clarion Books is an imprint of
Houghton Mifflin Harcourt Publishing Company.

www.hmhco.com

The illustrations in this book were done in India ink, watercolor, and colored pencil.
The text was set in Aged.

Library of Congress Cataloging-in-Publication Data
Names: Haeringen, Annemarie van, author, illustrator.
Title: How to knit a monster / Annemarie van Haeringen.
Other titles: Sneeuwwitje breit een monster. English
Description: Boston ; New York : Clarion Books/Houghton Mifflin Harcourt, 2018.
First published in the Netherlands in 2014 by Uitgeverij Leopold, Wibautstraat"–Title page verso.
Summary: When mean Mrs. Sheep insults Greta the goat's knitting, Greta quickly knits
a wolf that swallows Mrs. Sheep whole, but how will she get rid of the wolf?
Identifiers: LCCN 2017001025 | ISBN 9781328842107 (hardcover)
Subjects: | CYAC: Knitting–Fiction. | Goats–Fiction. | Sheep–Fiction. | Monsters–Fiction.
Classification: LCC PZ7.H11913 How 2018 | DDC [E]–dc23
LC record available at https://lccn.loc.gov/2017001025

Manufactured in China
SCP 10 9 8 7 6 5 4 3 2 1
4500708427

For Michael

Greta is a goat, a white goat. When she goes outdoors in wintertime, she's almost invisible.

She is a very, very good knitter. She knits socks for everyone she knows and for many she doesn't know.

Today Greta decides to knit something different.
How about a whole goat?

She tries a little one first.

Click, click, clickety click go her knitting needles,
and before long a little goat slides off her needle.

What fun! Greta knits more little goats so they
can play together.

Mean Mrs. Sheep marches into Greta's house.
"I'm a much better knitter than you!" she says.
"Much faster, and my work is more beautiful.
You knit too loosely. You drop stitches. What
on earth are you knitting now? What a mess!"
Greta is upset. She isn't watching her knitting.

We'll see who knits the fastest, Greta thinks angrily. Clickclickclicketyclick go her needles.

Mrs. Sheep keeps talking. Greta still isn't watching her knitting.

She decides it's finished and ends it off . . .

. . . and a wolf jumps off the needle!
The little goats run away.

He gobbles up Mrs. Sheep, wool and all.

Greta runs into the storage closet just
in time, before the wolf can gobble her up too.
Now what?

She has an idea.

In the closet she hastily knits a tiger:
clickclickclicketyclick!

She kicks the tiger out of the closet.

The tiger gobbles up the wolf, fur and all.

What's that noise?

It's the tiger, lying outside the closet door and licking his chops.

"I smell a succulent goatie," he mutters. "I'll have goat for dinner."

Greta is afraid.

I have to get rid of him! What should I knit now? she wonders.

Something even bigger, something even more dangerous!

Clickclickclicketyclick go the needles.

The tiger is still muttering. "Succulent goatie . . ."

Something is growing on Greta's needles.

Something big.

Something dangerous.

A MONSTER!

Greta is smart.

This time, she keeps the last stitches on her needle.

She pushes the monster out of the closet, but she doesn't let go of its tail!

The monster gobbles up the tiger, fur and all.

Then Greta pulls the monster back.

Riffle raffle riffle raffle whoosh: she unravels her knitting.

Riffle raffle riffle raffle—first the monster—*riffle raffle riffle raffle*—then the tiger, and finally—*riffle raffle riffle raffle whoosh*—the wolf.

And there is Mrs. Sheep!

"Sorry, sorry, sorry, Greta," she says. "You are a great, great knitter! So fast. So even. Such beautiful work!"

Greta smiles.

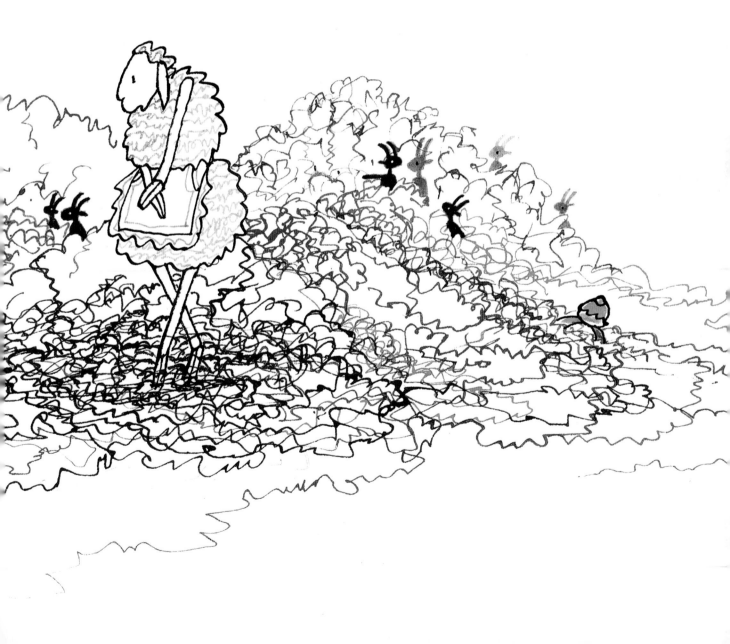

After Mrs. Sheep goes home, Greta puts
new stitches on her needles.

What next?

I know, thinks Greta. *I can knit some fresh
green grass for the little goats!*

She daydreams happily about the little
goats playing on the grass, and guess what?

She doesn't watch her knitting . . .